Alaina
and the Great Play

Written by **ELOISE GREENFIELD**

Illustrated by **COLIN BOOTMAN**

Alazar PRESS

Carrboro, North Carolina

To the memory of actress and writer, Ruby Dee,
and to all who love theater.
— ELOISE GREENFIELD

To the children of the world who have adapted
to change, with courage, during the covid-19 era.
This book is also dedicated to the loving memory
of my uncle, Wilfred Patrick St. Louis, who has
always been as source of inspiration and
encouragement for me.
— COLIN BOOTMAN

Text copyright 2021 by Eloise Greenfield
Illustrations copyright 2021 by Colin Bootman

Book design and production by Richard Hendel
Text edited by Jacqueline K. Ogburn

Library of Congress Cataloging-in-Publication Data
Names: Greenfield, Eloise, author. | Bootman, Colin, illustrator.
Title: Alaina and the great play / written by Eloise Greenfield ;
  illustrated by Colin Bootman.
Description: First edition. | Carrboro, North Carolina : Alazar Press,
  2021. | Audience: Ages 8-9. | Audience: Grades K-1. | Summary:
  Kindergartner Alaina is excited about thanking the audience at the end
  of the second-grade play, but she is overwhelmed by the performance and
  has to share her enthusiasm, center stage.
Identifiers: LCCN 2020034497 (print) | LCCN 2020034498 (ebook) | ISBN
  9781733686525 (cloth) | ISBN 9781733686532 (ebook)
Subjects: CYAC: Theater—Fiction. | Enthusiasm—Fiction. |
  Schools—Fiction. | Mothers and daughters—Fiction. | African
  Americans—Fiction.
Classification: LCC PZ7.G845 AL 2021 (print) | LCC PZ7.G845 (ebook) | DDC
  [E]—dc23
LC record available at https://lccn.loc.gov/2020034497
LC ebook record available at https://lccn.loc.gov/2020034498

ISBN 978-1-7336865-2-5
First Edition, 2021
Alazar Press is an imprint of Royal Swan Enterprises, Inc.
201 Orchard Lane, Carrboro, NC 27510
Visit us at *www.alazar-press.com*

Printed in Canada

That morning, when I felt myself waking up, I wasn't a bit happy about it. I wanted to sleep some more.

"Not yet," I said to myself, and I kept my eyes closed.

But then I heard my mom coming up the steps,

singing the song she made up about me — "Alaina, my

Alaina, my beautiful Alaina," and I knew that sleep time

was over.

Mom came into the room and kissed my forehead

and patted my shoulder.

"Time to get up," she said.

I said, "No-o-o-o."

"Yes," Mom said.

When she went out of the room, I pushed my face down deep into the

pillow for just a minute before I opened my eyes and sat up. I thought about my

mom's words, "Time to get up," and they made me laugh. Mom said those same

words every morning, and they never sounded funny to me before. But today, I

laughed and stood up on the bed, and I jumped as high as I could.

"I'm up! I'm up!" I said, laughing kind of loud. "I'm *waaay* up in the air!"

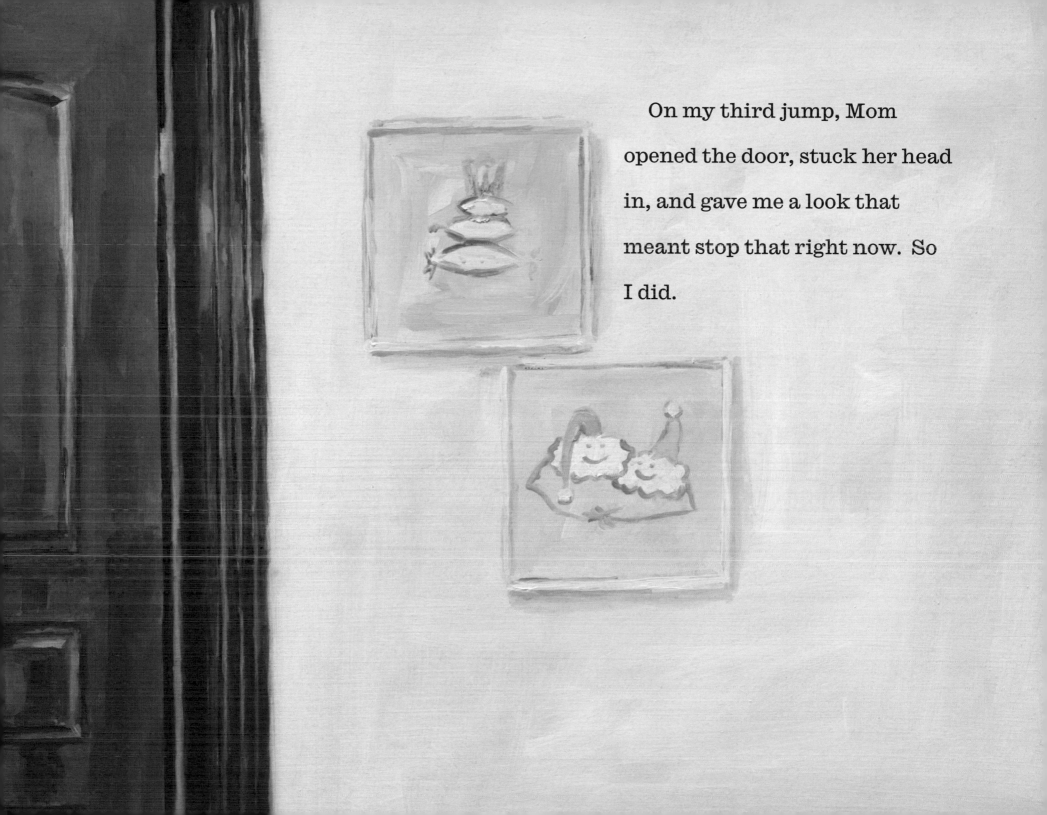

On my third jump, Mom opened the door, stuck her head in, and gave me a look that meant stop that right now. So I did.

Then I remembered what day it was and what was going to happen at school. The second-graders' play! And even though I'm only in kindergarten, I was going to make a speech at the end. It was only a little speech, five little words, but I couldn't wait to say them.

I hurried and took my bath, and I hurried and put on my new jeans and T-shirt, and I ate my breakfast and brushed my teeth extra fast.

On the way to school, I wanted Mom to walk faster. "We have to hurry up, Mom," I said. "The play!"

"The play's not until this afternoon," Mom said. "Why don't you practice your speech while we're walking?"

"Okay, here's my speech." I said, "Thank you for coming. Goodbye."

"That was great, Alaina," Mom said.

"It was?" I said. "Was it really, really, *really* great? Was it *stupendous*?"

I like to say that word. My dad says that about me all the time.

"Absolutely," Mom said. She said Dad couldn't get off from work to see the play, but I could tell him all about it when he got home.

When Mom and I got to my classroom door, she waved goodbye to me and to my teacher. "I'll be back to see the play," she said.

In our class, Mr. Hill read a story to us and asked us questions about it. Then we played a game, but I wasn't really listening to any of that. I was listening to my speech going around and around in my head.

After lunch, Miss Wheeler came to take me to the room behind the stage. On the way, I said, "Do you want to hear me say my speech?" I didn't wait for her to answer. I said, "Thank you for coming. Goodbye."

"Very good, Alaina," Miss Wheeler said.

In the room, the second-grade kids were ready to start the play. They were already dressed like college kids. They had on jeans and T-shirts with big letters on the front, and the girls had on lipstick and long earrings. They all went out on the stage, carrying books and backpacks, and then Miss Wheeler opened the curtains.

I stood right behind the curtains, so I could watch the play and the audience, too, but the people in the audience couldn't see me.

The kids on the stage started laughing and talking, acting like they were happy college friends. They teased each other and told jokes. The audience was laughing, too, and so was I, but I put my hand over my mouth, so nobody could hear me.

Then the friends had a big argument. They were all mad at each other, and they were yelling and saying mean things. I wanted them to stop, because they looked like they were mad for real, not like when I saw them practice.

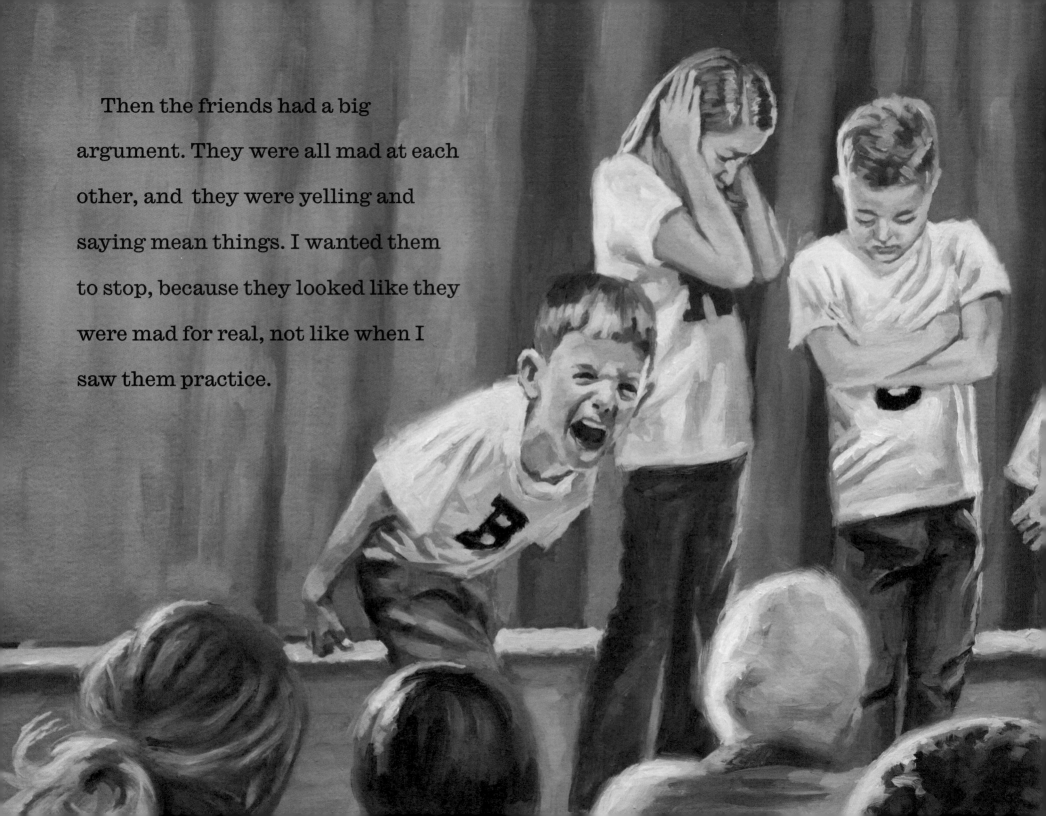

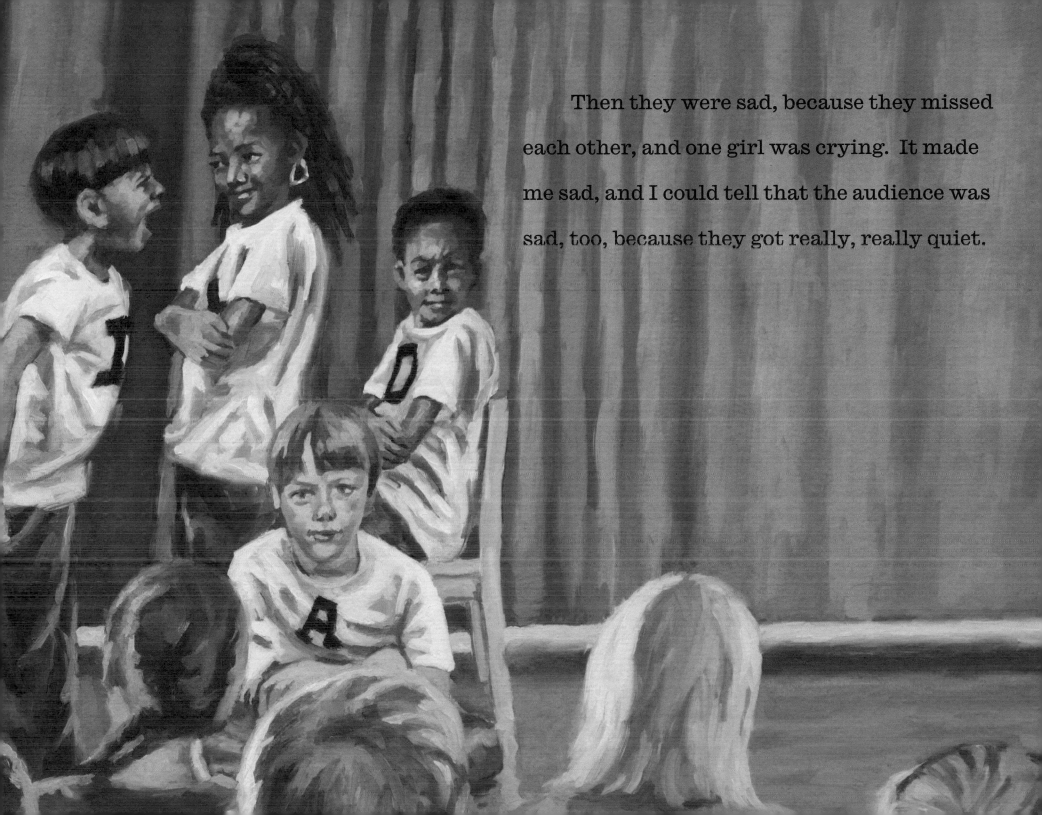

Then they were sad, because they missed each other, and one girl was crying. It made me sad, and I could tell that the audience was sad, too, because they got really, really quiet.

Then, after a while, the friends stopped being mad, and they were happy again. They were so happy, that they had a party. They played music and danced, and they were still dancing while Miss Wheeler closed the curtains really, really slow, and the play was over.

I wanted to be at that party. I was as happy as they were, because they liked each other again. The curtains opened again, and the kids bowed, and the audience stood up and clapped and clapped and clapped.

Then, Miss Wheeler waved me out on the stage to say my speech. But when I opened my mouth, the right words didn't come out. I was too excited to say that little speech. It wasn't good enough for that great play, so I lifted my arms up high and I spread them wide, and I said really loud, "Wasn't that great? Wasn't it *stupendous*? What about those jokes, and the yelling, and the crying, and the dancing, and . . . ?"

I saw Miss Wheeler behind the curtains, waving at me to come off the stage, but she didn't look mad. She looked a little bit tickled and a little bit serious at the same time, so I couldn't make myself behave.

The audience was clapping again, and I could tell that this time, they were clapping for me, and then I got *really* excited. I didn't know what to do next, so I did a somersault, and another one. And another one.

When I stood up, I saw the curtains closing, so I ran to the curtains and stuck my head out, and I said, in my loudest voice, "Thank you for coming! Goodbye!"

After the curtains were closed all the way, Miss Wheeler hugged us all and told us how good we were. When she hugged me, she laughed and shook her head and hugged me again.

On the way home, my mom put her arm around my shoulder. I was

hoping that other kids on their way home weren't paying any attention to us

and thinking that she was treating me like a baby. I wanted Mom to move her

arm away, but at the same time, I *didn't* want her to move it, because it made

me happy.

So many happy things happened that day, starting with my being waaay up in the air. I was thinking that every day should start just like that. But then I remembered Mom's look, and I told myself that, no, I'd better leave that part out. But the one thing I couldn't leave out was the play, because watching that great play was the best thing of all.